LULU

THE COCKER SPANIEL

A Story By

Kristin Stiff

Illustrated by Meredith Hancock

To: Claire

Lulu ♥'s you,

Kristin Stiff

CREDITS

Written by
Kristin Stiff

Illustrated by Meredith Hancock

Edited by Frank Monahan
Art Direction by Meredith Hancock

Published by Rocket Science Productions

ISBN-13: 978-1-937121-27-3

Library of Congress Control Number: 2012946135

Dedication

This book is dedicated to my parents, Chris and Gina Stiff, who inspire me every day to write.
Thank you for never giving up on my dream and for pushing me to do my best.
As a little girl, you heard my potential and allowed me to read it to you every day of my life.
I love you both!

I want to also dedicate this book to my husband, Marc, for supporting each and every
endeavor I take and for recognizing that our life together is an adventure.
Thank you for always having my best interest at heart. I love you.

I also give my love to my sister's, Kasey and Lacy (a.k.a. Lulu).
Thank you, Kasey, for being my role model, for standing as an inspiration to so many kids.
Thank you, Lulu, for allowing me to write my first book about your grand adventure.

Last but not least I dedicate my book to my grandparents.
Thank you Grandma and Grandpa Blinson for telling me to be true to myself!
Thank you Grandma and Grandpa Stiff for showing me that hard work is the key to success!

Love always,
Kristin

Lulu, the cocker spaniel, asleep in her bed,

awakes with a jolt, her alarm clock by her head.

1

Lulu, a proper spaniel, ready to begin her day,

yawns and stretches, bends down into a large plié.

Bounding out of her bed and into the shower,

Lulu soaks in the water for an entire hour.

3

Fresh is she that Lulu kisses the air,

then looks into the mirror brushing her hair.

Breakfast is ready; she can't wait to eat,

sitting at her bowl, she sees a slab of meat.

Washing her bowl, then running up the stairs,

Lulu howls a song and barks a prayer.

Flossing her teeth, then brushing them twice,

Lulu feels refreshed, she feels quite nice.

Skipping from the bathroom into her playroom,

Lulu hops about, jumping into her magical costume.

With a ruffled pink tutu, a magical wand in paw,

Lulu sits at her toy chest, staring at it in awe.

Her toy chest is miraculous, as she opens and finds,

a rubber bunny rabbit licking his behind!

9

"Ooo Noo!" exclaims Lulu, "you are not well,

if you do not stop licking, I will have to yell!"

"Please don't yell," says the bunny rabbit, "PLEASE!"

"For if you yell, you will wake the baby bumble bees!"

"Ooo Noo!" yells Lulu, "I am afraid of the bumbles,

every time I make a noise, they begin to rumble!"

"BUZZ BUZZ BUZZ," say the baby bumble bees,

"Yes! The toy chest is open, we are finally FREEE!"

Swooping over Lulu's head, the bees fly out,

Lulu ducks down quickly, and then begins to pout.

She demands the baby bumbles to fly back inside;

the babies become so scared that they escape and hide.

13

BOING goes Freddy the Frog, over the bunny;

he jumps so high, that he lands kind of funny.

"Ouch!" exclaims the frog, "I hurt my head."

"You should have stayed inside," says Lulu, "silly Fred!"

Flying over head, the bumbles are BAACK,

ready NOOW for a sweet savory snack.

Out pops a bone from Lulu's toy chest,

covered in peanut butter, it looks like a mess.

"Watch out!" cries the rabbit, "here come the beeees!"

The poor lonely bone falls down to its knees;

I am but plastic, I do not break,

so if you eat me, you will get a toothache.

My plastic is hard, my peanut butter tasty,

slow your flight; no need to be hasty.

The baby bumbles made no sound, not an utter,

swarming low, they stuck to the bone's peanut butter.

Shaking his poor body, the bone's in a tizzy.

So much that he falls from being too dizzy.

Lulu licks the peanut butter from the bone,

then calls for help on her cellular phone.

When no help arrives, Freddy makes a decision,

"NO TIME TO SPARE, no need for a division."

Freddy sticks out his long tongue with ease,

and slurps up the peanut butter bone and bees.

"YUMMY!" cries Freddy, "That tasted great!

The peanut butter wazz a beeutiful bait."

Lulu is sad, she lost a friend,

"I cannot believe that was his end."

After all the trouble the toy chest caused,

Lulu jumps on it with her two front paws.

Freddy, the frog said to the trembling bunny,

"The bees I ate tasted nothing like honey."

Lulu waves her magical wand above her head,

then spins around, twirling the wand at Fred.

The plump, pitiful Frog turns very green,

"My stomach is swishing like a washing machine!"

The rubber bunny rabbit closes her eyes,

but when she opens them, she sees a wonderful surprise.

The bees were buzzing and the bone was alive;

Bone squealed, "Hurray," then gave Lulu a high five.

Freddy's stomach felt better and his color came back.

He learned to choose wiser when picking a snack.

"I'll stick to grass and mud pies and such,

and I won't interfere if a situation is too much."

Lulu sighs aloud and flops to the ground,

then howls a tune like a silly basset hound.

Her day was filled with much surprise,

so Lulu decides to say her goodbyes.

"Dear extraordinary friends, you have been a riot,

and I'm glad that Freddy's on a bone-free diet."

All the toys leaped back in the magical box,

before Lulu fastened it with several big locks.

Out of her pink tutu and away from the playroom,

Lulu dashes to school in a hurry, ZOOOMMM.

She went to Art, Math, Science, and History,

and in English class wrote a very good mystery.

In P.E. she played basketball and bowled,

and Lulu did exactly what she was told.

Her P.E. teacher, Mrs. Moo Moo, said to the class,

"It's not nice to poke fun at animals with gas.

The class before last I heard Owl weeping,

because she tooted twice in the middle of leaping.

It caused such a scene, as the animals heard,

and Lulu was the only one that said not a word."

"Thank you sweet Lulu for being my friend,

after I hooted a toot from the opposite end."

Lulu turned to her P.E. class with a sassy 'tude,

and said very loud, "You guys were rude!

Today I learned from my magical toy chest,

that you shouldn't eat what you can't digest."

At the end of the school day Lulu said,

"I am so very tired and ready for bed!"

As she trotted to her house and in the door,

Lulu plopped on her bed and began to snore.

About the Author

Kristin Stiff lives in Newport News, Virginia with her husband Marc, and a rambunctious Cane Corso, Prince. As a graduate of the University of Virginia with a major in English, Kristin has learned a thing or two about writing. As a little girl, Kristin wrote many whimsical tales, hoping one day to be a published author. Kristin was certain after her first year of college, eight years ago, that her precious Cocker Spaniel sister, Lacy (a.k.a. Lulu), was going to be the main character of her first book.

Kristin and Lulu spend many wonderful hours together, sunbathing at the beach, curling their hair, and eating their favorite treats. They go on many adventures together that have inspired this book! When Kristin is not writing, she is swimming, running, and going to the gym. Her fitness is an asset to her writing, as she develops a lot of ideas while exercising.

More books available from RSP

You can purchase all of these books directly from the publisher at
shop.rsp-llc.com (preferred) or at Amazon.com